Puzzle Balloon Race

Rosie Heywood

Designed and illustrated by
Brenda Haw

Edited by Felicity Brooks

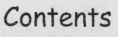

Contents

2 Puzzle Balloon Race   18 Professor Inflator's house

4 Getting ready   20 Dimply Desert

6 In the air   22 Compost Farm

8 Steamy Jungle   24 Cactus Gully

10 Towers Town   26 Fountain School

12 High mountain peaks   28 Prize party

14 Swampy Islands   30 The next day

16 Brainstorm Valley   31 Answers

Puzzle Balloon Race

Ben and his cousin Jess are young aeronauts, learning how to fly hot air balloons.

Ben's Uncle John has entered the Puzzle Balloon Race and he's asked Ben and Jess to help him. Uncle John hasn't been an aeronaut for long. Sometimes he forgets how to fly the balloon, so he'll need to take the Balloon Instruction Book with him.

Uncle John has sent Ben and Jess the race rules, and pictures of three other racers.

Ricky Pickles. His balloon has red and blue stripes.

Race rules

Each team must take off from Airlift Field and fly their balloon to the finish. On the way they must photograph:

A crinkly cactus flower from Cactus Gully.

A Jungle Jangle bird from the Steamy Jungle.

The tallest tower in Towers Town.

A swampy rabbit from Swampy Islands.

Compost Farm's prize-winning cow.

The first team to reach the finish with their photos will be the winners.

PS Rattling snakes like to eat chocolate.

PPS Watch out for storm puff birds. They glide on the Queasy Squall, a dangerous wind.

Amy Airspace. Her balloon is yellow with green spots.

Bob Balloonburster and Sneaky. Their balloon has white stars on it. Sneaky is hiding on each double page.

There are puzzles on every page. See if you can solve them all and help Ben, Jess and Uncle John win the Puzzle Balloon Race. If you get stuck, the answers are on pages 31 and 32.

Here's a page from the Balloon Instruction Book.

How to fly your balloon

1. Use the burners to fill the balloon with hot air. It will start to rise because hot air is lighter than cool air.

2. To keep going up, use short blasts of the burners to keep the air hot.

3. To go down, stop blasting the burners to let the air cool.

4. Your balloon will go where the wind takes it. If you go up and down, you can catch winds blowing in different directions.

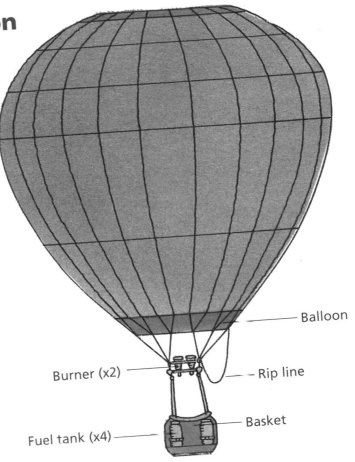

Balloon

Burner (x2) — Rip line

Fuel tank (x4) — Basket

Flight instruments to help you fly your balloon

Compass - tells you which direction you're flying in.

Cold Hot

Temperature gauge - tells you how hot the balloon is.

12.5 KMPH

Ballooning calculator - tells you how fast you are going.

682.9 METRES

Altimeter - tells you how high you are.

Full Empty

Fuel gauge - tells you how much fuel you have left.

Top tips
Pull the rip line if you need to go down quickly.
If the balloon overheats, stop blasting the burners until the temperature drops.

Getting ready

The day of the race has arrived at last. When they reach Airlift Field, Uncle John, Ben and Jess carefully unpack the balloon and lay it on the ground.

They fasten the burners to the basket and make sure they work.

They lower the basket onto its side and attach it to the balloon.

They blow the balloon up with cold air first, using a fan.

Then they start to heat the air by blasting the burners.

"Are we ready for takeoff?" asks Ben.

"Nearly," replies Uncle John, looking around the field. "But I don't think I've remembered to pack everything. I've put the flight instruments in the basket, but we also need the instant camera, two maps, the rope ladder, the lunch box and three bottles of lemonade."

Can you find the things they need?

Uncle John has forgotten something else important.

Do you know what it is?

5

In the air

As hot air fills the balloon, Uncle John, Jess and Ben climb into the basket. It can't drift too far because Jess has tied it to a post.

"When the starter blows the whistle we can untie the rope and start the race!" says Uncle John.

They are floating high in the air when he realizes they've forgotten the Balloon Instruction Book.

"We'll have to go down and get it," he sighs. "There should be time before the race begins."

"Look!" shouts Ben. "I can see Amy Airspace's balloon! And Ricky Pickles'... and Bob Balloonburster's."

Can you see them too?

"Come on Ben, we'd better check the fuel tanks," says Jess.

Each full tank has enough fuel for two hours of flying. All the tanks are full, so how long can the balloon fly for?

Steamy Jungle

Uncle John, Jess and Ben are ready to race at last. The starter blows the whistle and they begin to fly. Soon they can see the Steamy Jungle.

"We'll never spot the Jungle Jangle bird from up here," says Ben. "I'll have to climb down the ladder."

"Remember it has a yellow beak, purple wings, and a very long tail," says Uncle John.

"Good luck!" calls Jess. "Tie the rope to a safe branch or we might float off without you!"

Towers
Town

Ben climbs down the ladder, ties the rope to a branch and looks around. Where is the Jungle Jangle bird?

Can you spot the Jungle Jangle bird?

As soon as he has taken a photograph of the Jungle Jangle bird, Ben rushes back to where he's tied the balloon. But it has gone! From somewhere above the trees, he can hear Uncle John calling to him.

Why has the balloon disappeared?

Towers Town

When Uncle John and Jess reach Towers Town, the balloon suddenly stops.

"What's happened?" asks Jess. Uncle John leans out of the balloon to have a look.

"We're stuck," he says. "We forgot to pull the ladder up and now it's caught around the top of a tower!"

"Don't worry," says Jess. "Ben can untangle the ladder before he climbs back into the balloon."

"I hope Ben gets here soon," says Uncle John. "Because Ricky Pickles has overtaken us."

Can you see where Ben is?

While they wait for Ben to reach them, Jess checks the flight instruments.

"Look at the altimeter," she says. "We're losing height. If we sink much lower, we'll start hitting the towers."

What should they do to make the balloon rise?

High mountain peaks

Ben untangles the ladder and climbs into the balloon. Jess takes a photo of the tallest tower. Soon they can see some mountains.

"We're four hundred metres up," says Uncle John. "We need to reach eight hundred metres to fly over the mountains. Each burner blast lifts us fifty metres. How many blasts do we need?"

How many blasts do you think they need?

Before Jess and Ben have time to reply, the balloon begins to shake.

"Hang on tight!" shouts Uncle John. "It must be the Queasy Squall!"

When the wind finally dies down, everything looks very different.

Can you spot all the differences?

Swampy Islands

The balloon rises higher and higher until it floats over the mountaintops. Soon Ben and Jess can see the Swampy Islands. After they've landed, Jess ties the rope around a rock, while Uncle John and Ben start looking for swampy rabbits.

"I can see them on the far island," says Ben.

"Some of the bridges are broken," says Jess. "We'll have to choose our route very carefully."

Can you find a safe route to the rabbits?

I don't like the look of those crocodiles!

They photograph one of the rabbits, then rush back to the balloon.
As it begins to rise, Uncle John looks confused.

"I need to know which direction we're flying in," he says, "but I
can't remember which flight instrument to look at."

Can you remember which flight instrument shows direction?

Brainstorm Valley

Jess looks at the flight instruments. "We're heading south," she says.

"Good," says Uncle John. "That means we're over Brainstorm Valley and on our way to the Dimply Desert. But we've got a problem - the burners have stopped working and we're going down!"

"I think someone damaged them while we were looking for the swampy rabbits," says Ben. "And I've found this clue."

Do you know who damaged the burners?

Jess starts flicking through the Balloon Instruction Book. Professor Inflator, the balloon inventor, lives in Brainstorm Valley. She should be able to help them. Suddenly Jess finds what she needs - a map.

"Quick," she says. "Let's land at Professor Inflator's house."

Can you see which is Professor Inflator's house?

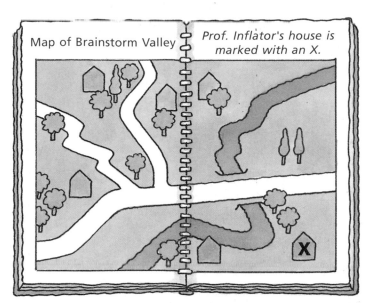

Map of Brainstorm Valley

Prof. Inflator's house is marked with an X.

Professor Inflator's house

Jess, Ben and Uncle John knock on Professor Inflator's door.
When she answers, they tell her about the broken burners.

"I'll be able to mend your burners," says Professor Inflator. "But before
I do, can you help me find my floppy disks? I've found this green
one, but there are also three blue, three red, and two yellow disks."

Jess and Ben look around the messy room. It isn't going
to be easy, and they will have to hurry if they
still want to win the race.

Can you find all the disks?

Around the World Balloons

Green balloon
Upward force = 360 N
Downward force = 250 N

Blue balloon
Upward force = 450 N
Downward force = 300 N

Purple balloon
Upward force = 265 N
Downward force = 200 N

Force is measured in Newtons (N)

"The other disks have information on them about my three new balloons," says Professor Inflator. "I need to take the downward force of each balloon away from its upward force. The one with the most upward force left should be able to fly around the world!"

Do you know which balloon will be able to fly around the world?

Dimply Desert

As soon as Professor Inflator has mended the burners, they are ready to take off. Before long, they are floating over the Dimply Desert.

"We're moving really fast," says Uncle John. "I think we could still win the race!"

Suddenly another balloon zooms past them. It's Bob Balloonburster.

How is Bob Balloonburster managing to go so fast?

"I'm going to take a photo of Bob Balloonburster's balloon," says Ben. "I don't think they'll let him win when they see what he's been up to."

"Good idea," says Uncle John. "Meanwhile, can you help me, Jess? Our speed is twelve kilometres per hour and Compost Farm is six kilometres away. I need to know how long it will take us to get there."

How long do you think it will take them to get to Compost Farm?

Compost Farm

Jess, Ben and Uncle John just have time to eat their lunch before they arrive at Compost Farm. They can see a patchwork of fields below them, but where is the prize-winning cow?

"Which field is your prize-winning cow in?" Jess shouts to Farmer Compost.

"Daisy? She's in a field with two apple trees," calls Farmer Compost. "She's brown with black spots."

Can you find Daisy?

"We're too high up to photograph Daisy," says Ben. "I think I know how to go down quickly, but I'd better check in the Balloon Instruction Book first."

Can you remember how to make the balloon go down quickly?

Cactus Gully

After they've photographed Daisy, they float on to Cactus Gully. It's too dangerous to land, because of the prickly spines, so Ben and Jess climb down the ladder. They can see the crinkly cactus flower in the distance, but the path is blocked by rattling snakes.

"How can we get past the rattling snakes?" says Ben.

"We need to feed them," says Jess, reaching into her pocket. "And I've got something they like."

Can you remember what rattling snakes like to eat?

"We've got one full tank of fuel left," says Uncle John, as Ben and Jess climb back into the balloon. "How much longer can we stay in the air?"

Do you know the answer to Uncle John's question?

Fountain School

Uncle John, Jess and Ben now have all the photographs they need. Uncle John looks carefully at the map and the flight instruments.

"Our speed is eight kilometres per hour and the finish is two kilometres away. How long will it take us to get there?" he asks.

Jess and Ben soon know the answer.

Do you know how long it will take them to reach the finish?

Ben and Jess can see their friends below them in the school playground. They are holding up cards with letters on.

"It's a message for us," says Jess, "but they've muddled up the letters."

Do you know what the message should say?

Prize party

Jess leans out of the basket. Far below them, the ground is whizzing past. In the distance, she can see the finish.

"If we keep going at this speed," says Uncle John, "we could win the race!"

As they reach the finish, Uncle John stops blasting the burners.

The balloon skims over some tree-tops, and lands with a bump.

The basket tips over and Ben, Jess and Uncle John tumble out.

They can hardly believe it. They've won the Puzzle Balloon Race!

Soon other balloons begin to land. Everybody cheers as Uncle John, Ben and Jess go up to collect their prize medals.

"Thank you so much for helping me," says Uncle John to Ben and Jess. "I couldn't have won the race without you."

Ricky Pickles, Amy Airspace and Bob Balloonburster haven't finished the race yet.

Do you know why? (You'll have to look back through the book to find out what's happened to them.)

The next day

The following morning at Uncle John's house, Ben and Jess write about the Puzzle Balloon Race in their flight notebooks.

"If we flew eighty kilometres in eight hours," Ben mutters to himself, "what was our average speed?"

Do you know what their average speed was?

Jess sighs happily. What an amazing race it had been. Just then, she looks up and sees a huge balloon floating in the sky.

Do you know who the balloon belongs to and where it's going?

Answers

Pages 4-5 Getting ready

The things that Uncle John needs are circled here.

He's forgotten the Balloon Instruction Book.

Pages 6-7 In the air

The balloons are marked here.

Uncle John's balloon can fly for eight hours.

Pages 8-9 Steamy Jungle

The Jungle Jangle bird is circled here.

The balloon disappeared because the branch snapped.

Pages 10-11 Towers Town

Ben is circled here.

They should blast the burners to make the balloon rise.

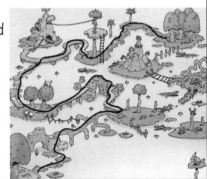

Pages 12-13 High mountain peaks

They need eight blasts of the burners.

The differences are shown here.

Pages 14-15 Swampy Islands

The route to the rabbits is marked in black.

The compass shows direction (page 3).

Pages 16-17 Brainstorm Valley

Sneaky damaged the burners.

Professor Inflator's house is circled here.

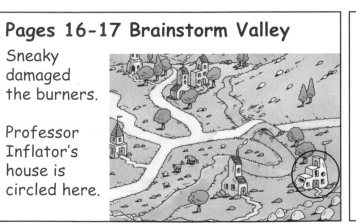

Pages 18-19 Prof. Inflator's house

The floppy disks are marked here.

The around-the-world balloon is the one in the middle.

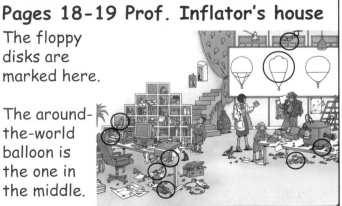

Answers

Pages 20-21 Dimply Desert

Bob Balloonburster has turbo jets on his balloon.

It will take them 30 minutes to get to Compost Farm.

Pages 22-23 Compost Farm

The prize-winning cow is circled here.

They need to pull the rip line to go down fast (page 3).

Pages 24-25 Cactus Gully

Rattling snakes like to eat chocolate (page 2).

The balloon can stay in the air for two hours (page 7).

Pages 26-27 Fountain School

It will take them 15 minutes to reach the finish.

The message should say GOOD LUCK!

Pages 28-29 Prize party

Ricky Pickles crash landed in the Dimply Desert (page 21).

Amy Airspace was chased by a bull at Compost Farm (page 23).

Bob Balloonburster landed on a cactus in Cactus Gully (page 25).

Page 30 The next day

Their average speed was 10 kilometres per hour.

The balloon Jess has spotted is Professor Inflator's (page 19). It's going around the world.

Sneaky puzzle

Did you remember to look out for Bob Balloonburster's wicked spy Sneaky?
He was hiding somewhere on every double page.

This edition first published in 2005 by Usborne Publishing Ltd, 83-85 Saffron Hill, London EC1N 8RT, England. Copyright © 2005, 1999 Usborne Publishing Ltd. www.usborne.com.
The name Usborne and the devices ♀ 🌐 are Trade Marks of Usborne Publishing Ltd.